To the staff of Young Life,
experts on loving kids

Pumpkin, how come he doesn't play with us anymore?

And why does he wear dark glasses all the time?

He said his new friends are "dudes." I'm a dude, aren't I?

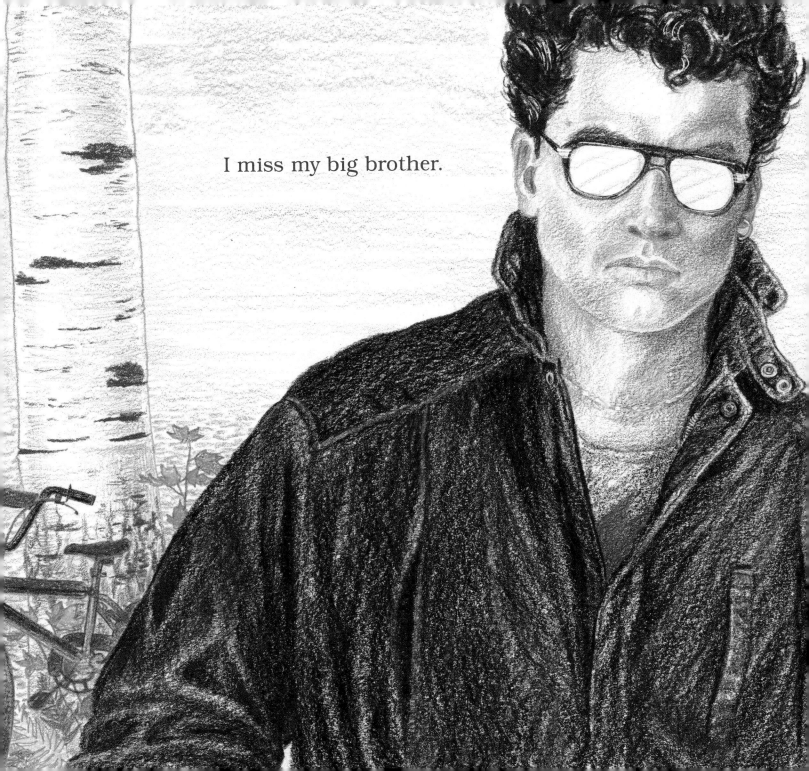

I miss my big brother.

I heard Daddy yelling at Mommy,

"You tell *me* where the money went then! I say Craig took it."

And Mommy said, "He wouldn't do that; you're just mad because his grades have dropped and he's skipping school."

Just last night Mommy said she didn't think Craig was feeling well. That's why he took naps every afternoon and had such a blank expression on his face and was *soooo* pale.

Now she said, "At least he's not doing drugs!"

"Why are you going out now, Craig?"

"Look kid, you open your mouth and you're dead meat! I'm gonna make a deal, that's all."

"You mean drugs, Craig? You're going to get drugs? When Mom asked if you were using drugs, you said 'no' and she was so happy."

I'm scared, Pumpkin.
Craig's the boss, not
Mommy and Daddy.

"Hey there David, tell your brother he better start showing up for football practice!"

"Yeah, coach, my brother's been sick."

"Say, where's your new bike?"

"Craig said that to *rat* on somebody is the worst thing of all, but I need to tell someone. He needed some money so he sold my bike. He said it's better to steal than deal. He's no addict. He said lots of kids use more than he does."

I love Craig.

Why is he using drugs?

"Hey, Craig, I saw you smoking pot."

"Yeah, little brother, so I get wasted with my friends. The music is better when I'm stoned."

"Mom asked why your room smells like burnt rope and why you use so much room deodorant. What should I tell her?"

"Tell her to back off. Stay out of my life!"

Pumpkin, he can't see how much
he has changed. Those guys
aren't his friends!

Craig yelled, "Gross . . . dog food for dinner!"

Daddy's face got all red and he said, "That's it, Craig. Leave the table!"

And Mom said, "If you'd lighten up, he'd be okay."

On his way out Craig laughed and said, "Yeah, Pop, lighten up. I've had one of those normal childhoods, you know . . . full of loneliness, guilt, pain and fear. So, lighten up."

When he left the room I said,
"I think it's the drugs that make
  him act like that."

"Drugs?" Mom said. Drugs?"

"Yes, Mom. For a long time."

Daddy said, "Well, he's gone. He took off when I told him we knew about the drugs."

And the coach said, "He won't be back tonight. He'll wait 'til you're worried sick and knows you'll be glad to see him."

"I see it all the time . . .
first, keg parties, . . .
then smoking some pot
thinking they can
handle it, then trying
some other drugs,
dropping non-using
friends, stealing to get
money, and . . ."

Craig shrugged, "So I got busted."

And Daddy said, "Talk English, Craig. What happened?"

The policeman interrupted and said he was arrested for breaking into a house and robbing it. He said they found drugs on him. Then he turned to Craig and said,

"I have some advice for you, young man:

#1 Stay away from places
where there are drugs.

#2 Change your friends.
Find some winners."

Craig said, "Hey, man, I can stop anytime I want to. I'm just having fun!"

And the officer muttered, "If only that were true. If only that were true."

YOU DON'T NEED DRUGS

Mom was crying, "How could you do this to us?

    You know better!
    After all we've done for you.
    Where did we go wrong?"

Daddy looked Craig straight in the eye and said, "Listen, son, things are going to be different from now on. To begin, you are grounded for one month, and that includes use of the phone."

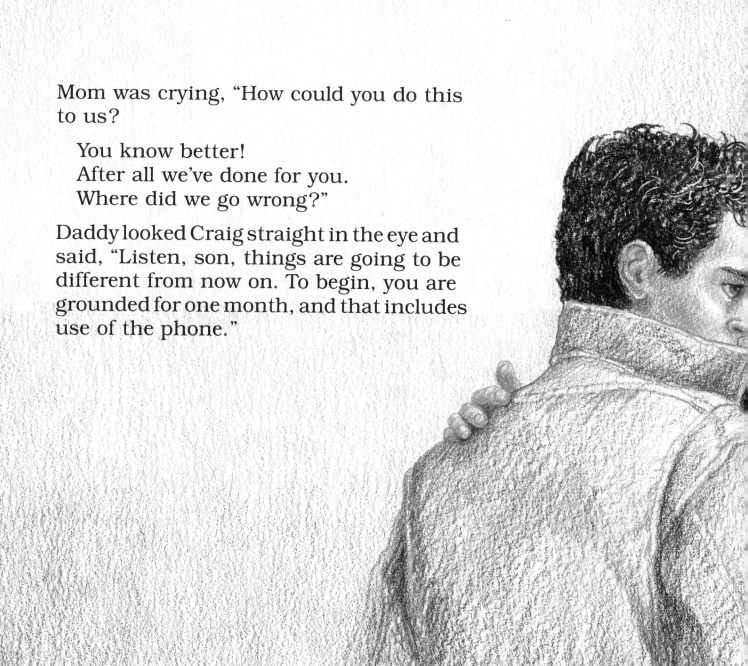

Don't be afraid to be strong,
Daddy. It makes me feel safe.

Craig has hurt himself and I'm
sorry for that.

He's hurt me, too, and that
makes me cry.

Know what, Pumpkin . . .

it's okay to say NO to drugs.

"Why does Craig use drugs?

  Because his friends use;
  Because his music encourages it;
  Because he likes the 'high';
  Because it makes him feel tough;
  Because he wants to hurt you;
  Because it's there;
  And a million other reasons.

"Tell Craig he cannot use drugs and live in your home. He needs clear, firm limits. When he can't control you anymore, look out!"

"Not until he is drug-free will he know what it has done to him."

"Now, David, I want to tell you something.
We are all very
proud of you.
Choosing to say no
to drugs
is very smart!"

Dear Friend,

By the time a child enters junior high school he will
be forced to say yes or no to drugs. There is no greater
motivation for kids to stay off drugs than a close,
loving family.

1. Give the child reasons not to use drugs.
2. Spend time regularly having fun with your child.
3. It is usually a friend who introduces drugs, not
   a stranger.
4. State clearly what will happen if he uses drugs.
5. Know where he is and who his friends are and
   what drugs are available at school.
6. Don't be afraid to be a strong parent and don't
   be afraid of your child.